# Family Matters

## Have No Fear, the Urk Man Is Here

D0104336

# *Family Matters*

### Have No Fear, the Urk Man Is Here

**by Bonnie Worth**

*Based on the series* FAMILY MATTERS, *created by*
**William Bickley & Michael Warren**

*and developed by*
**Thomas L. Miller & Robert L. Boyett**

*and on episodes written by*
**Fred Fox, Jr., Jim Geoghan, & Gary Goodrich**

**A PARACHUTE PRESS BOOK**

Parachute Press, Inc.
156 Fifth Avenue
New York, NY 10010

FAMILY MATTERS, characters, names and all related indicia are trademarks of
Lorimar Television © 1992.

Copyright © 1992 by Lorimar Television.

All rights reserved. No part of this book may be reproduced or transmitted in
any form or by any means, electronic or mechanical, including photocopying,
recording or by any information storage and retrieval system, without the
written permission of the Publisher, except where permitted by law.

ISBN: 0-938753-71-1
Printed in the United States of America
October 1992
10  9  8  7  6  5  4  3  2  1

# ONE

**CLICK. CLICK. WHRRRRR.**

The Winslows' front door opened a crack—just wide enough to admit a video camera. *Whrrrrr.*

Carl Winslow, the operator of the camera, soon followed, narrating as he entered the house.

"We are now entering the residence of one of Chicago's finest . . . police sergeant Carl Winslow." He panned the living room.

"There on the easy chair is his beloved daughter Laura," he continued. "She's an active member of her student council, an honor student, and a truly well-rounded individual. Takes after her old man, naturally." He chuckled modestly.

Laura looked up from her math book. "Neat camera, Dad," she said. "But no interviews now. I'm in the middle of a killer equation."

"That's my girl." Carl grinned and continued panning until he reached the couch. "This is the sergeant's youngest daughter, Judy the Couch Potato, watching the tube along with her couch potato cousin, Richie. Say, why aren't you kids outside playing in the fresh air?"

"Hey!" Richie said, turning away from the TV. "That's a neat camera, Uncle Carl. Can I play with it?"

Carl ignored him and continued narrating his home movie. He focused on a space next to the couch.

"This is the spot where Sergeant Winslow drops his police bag after a long, hard day of fighting crime."

Next, Carl focused the camera on an attractive young woman sitting at the desk. She seemed to be making some sort of list.

"And there she is, Carl's sister-in-law and Richie's mom, Rachel. Rachel is the sister—"

"Make that *baby sister*, please," Rachel said, looking up from her list. "And shoot me from this angle, please." She turned her head so that the camera got her "good" side. She had heard that all actors had one.

"Rachel is the *baby* sister," Carl corrected himself, "of Carl's lovely wife, Harriette, and owner and operator of Rachel's Place, a successful local restaurant—"

Rachel wagged a finger at him. "Actually, Carl, it's a snack shop."

"And speaking of snacks," Carl said, shifting the camera's focus to a certain gray-haired woman.

Mother Winslow looked up from her knitting and gave her son a look.

"This fine lady happens to be the world's finest snack maker. She is Sergeant Winslow's mommy. Hi, Mommy." He grinned fondly and waved from behind the camera.

"Why look," his mother replied smartly. "It's my lunatic son. Hi, son."

Carl lowered the camera, still as enthusiastic as a kid with a new toy. "Mother, isn't this a wonderful camera? I bought it at a police auction."

"Well, it's about time you splurged for something like this. How long did it take you to crowbar your wallet open?" she asked.

Carl grinned. "Very funny, Mother. I want you to know that this camera comes with a self-timer so if we do a family video, I can be in it."

"Then you'll need a wide-angle lens," she said dryly.

"Very funny!" Carl said, smirking. But she did have a point. Carl was on the chubby side. Having a mother who made the most delicious high-calorie snacks didn't help matters any.

Laura shook her head, baffled. "These algebra

equations are murder. I just don't get them."

"Maybe you should ask Professor Einstein next door to help you," Mother Winslow suggested.

Laura made a face. She knew exactly whom her grandmother meant by *Einstein*. None other than Steve Urkel, their next-door neighbor, who was just about the smartest kid in the school—and also the most obnoxious. Plus he had a crush on Laura. "No thanks," Laura said. "I think I'll muddle through myself . . . without Einstein-Urkel."

"Urkel?" Carl said, stiffening at the very mention of the name. "Yuck!" Urkel was not exactly high on Carl's list of people he liked to have around.

"Now, don't you be criticizing that young man," Mother Winslow scolded. The older women of the house had a soft spot for Steve, even if Laura and Carl did not. As far as Mother Winslow, Harriette, and Rachel were concerned, he was well-mannered and considerate—kind of like an old-fashioned boy. "That young man's got a fine head on his shoulders," Mother Winslow continued, "and he's a darned sight brighter than *some* males I can think of."

Just then Eddie, the oldest Winslow child, came in from the kitchen carrying a paper bag.

"Speaking of less bright," Laura muttered

when she saw her big brother.

"Hi, y'all," Eddie said glumly. What Eddie lacked in brainpower, he made up for in looks. He was tall, well built, and as handsome as a movie star. But it looked as if he was having a bad day.

"What's wrong, son?" Carl asked.

"Vonda just turned me down for a date . . . for the second time in two weeks. Do you think I could be losing my touch with women?"

"You, son?" Carl said. "Never."

Eddie didn't look convinced. "I've been thinking of changing my look. Maybe I should shave my initials onto the side of my head."

"Perfect, Eddie," Laura said without looking up from her book. "E. W. Stands for *eeeew!*"

"Laura," Eddie said, looking hurt, "I don't think you're taking this seriously."

"You're right," Laura agreed.

Eddie reached into his paper bag. "I was thinking maybe I should grow a mustache. Maybe that would attract women," he said. He took a false mustache out of the bag and held it under his nose. "What does this say to you? Sophisticated? Mature? . . . "

Laura looked up, unimpressed. "Try *bonehead*," she said bluntly.

Eddie pulled a pair of sunglasses out of the bag and tried them on. "What do you think about the cool look?"

"To tell you the truth," Carl said, "not much, son."

"Cool? It's more like lukewarm," Laura said.

But Eddie wasn't about to give up. He tried on a hat. "What does this say to you?"

"That you're desperate," Laura said. She wished he'd stop distracting her. She had to finish her math homework so she would have time to prepare some notes for tomorrow's Student Council meeting.

Eddie then fished a black beret out of the bag and set it on his head at a rakish angle. " 'Ow about ze beret?" he said in a French accent. "After all, France is ze land of romance."

"Eddie, you're hopeless in any language," Laura said. Then she got a gleam in her eye. "I have a great suggestion."

She got up, went over to her brother, took the paper bag out of his hand, and put it on over his head. "Now *that*," she said, sitting back down again, "improves your look."

"Hey," Eddie said from inside the bag, "let me out."

Just then, the front door swung open and a familiar, high-pitched voice sang out, "Have no fear, Eddo, my buddy—the Urk Man is here."

# TWO

**STEVE URKEL STRODE** across the living room, grabbed the front of the paper bag with both hands, and tore it along the center. Eddie could see again.

"No need to thank me, Eddo," Steve said gallantly. "Actually I've come here to ask *you* for a favor. But first . . ."

Steve turned to Laura, who was doing her best to disappear behind her math book. She was in no mood for Steve Urkel.

"Ah, Laura, you look lovely this evening," Steve said. "That algebra book becomes you. It goes with your hair. You certainly know the right books to wear."

Laura groaned as the goggle-eyed boy in horn-rimmed glasses made a corny bow in her direc-

7

tion. In addition to the horn-rims, he wore clunky saddle shoes, white socks, a varsity sweater, and red suspenders that hitched his gray dress pants up almost to his armpits—his usual outfit. It was no secret that Steve was in love with Laura. It was also no secret that Laura considered Steve a royal pain. When the school nerd had a raging crush on you, it was more of a handicap than a cause for celebration.

"Steve," Carl said with pretend sweetness, "don't you have something dangerous to do? Like disarm a nuclear reactor?"

Steve appeared to give this question serious thought. "Let's see . . . the nearest nuclear reactor is 15.6 miles away from here, as the crow flies, and, as far as I know, it is on-line and functioning without difficulties as of the most recent on-site inspection by a team from the Nuclear Regulatory Commission."

"I'm so happy to hear that," Carl said without sincerity as he edged toward the stairs. "Now, you'll excuse me while I go upstairs to film my lovely wife."

"Go to it, sir," Steve said respectfully. "I, myself, was just about to go into the kitchen to have a heart-to-heart talk with your eldest."

Eddie followed Steve into the kitchen. "Heart-to-heart?" Eddie repeated. He went to the refrigerator and took out a carton of milk and some caramel fudge Mother Winslow had whipped up the day before. Eddie had the appetite of a normal, healthy growing boy—awesome.

At that moment, a boy appeared at the window of the kitchen door and pressed his nose to the glass.

"Ah, if it isn't Waldo!" said Steve. "He must have smelled the fudge."

Waldo, Eddie's best friend, was a bit on the spacey side. In fact, compared to Waldo, Eddie could pass as a genius.

Eddie signaled to Waldo to come on in. Waldo seemed confused for a moment and pointed to himself quizzically. But finally realizing Eddie meant him, Waldo grinned and opened the door.

"What's happening?" he asked, heading straight for the plate of fudge. While the older boys dug in, Steve took a seat across the kitchen table from them. He wasn't hungry at the moment. He had other things on his mind.

"Eddie," Steve said, "I need you to help me."

Eddie chewed on the caramel fudge and nodded his head. "Sure thing. What with?"

"I need you to help Laura and me move along with our relationship."

Eddie stopped chewing. "I hate to be a downer here," he said, "but you and my sister don't *have* a relationship."

"I beg to differ, Edward, my fine fudgeomaniac

friend. She's been very grateful ever since I helped her ace the last algebra test. I even think she's been flirting with me."

The other two stared at Steve in disbelief.

"She has?" Waldo said.

"Oh yeah. Just the other night she actually telephoned me in the middle of the night."

"Steve, there was a fire in your kitchen," Eddie pointed out. "She happened to see it from her window."

Steve shrugged. "Still, she did call and save me from becoming a Crispy Critter. Anyway, Eddo, I need your advice. You know everything there is to know about the fair sex."

Eddie puffed his chest out in pride, forgetting his recent bad luck with Vonda. "You're right about that."

"I want you to tell me how to win a lady's heart. I mean," Steve said, moving his chair closer to Eddie, "what really works?"

"Well," Eddie began, "based on my vast personal experience, there are two things that really work. The first is . . ."

Steve leaned forward. He respected Eddie's advice when it came to women. Eddie was very popular, and Steve was ready to hear anything he had to say.

" . . . share their interests," Eddie finished.

Steve leaned back, disappointed. He was expecting to hear Eddie's personal secrets on grooming, clothing, colognes—or even on how to put over the smoothest of moves. But "share their interests"? Was this guy pulling his leg?

Eddie nodded solemnly. "Works every time."

"Like when?" Waldo wondered.

"You know Laverne Skinner?" Eddie asked them.

They nodded.

"President of the chess club," said Steve.

"President of the chess club *and* foxiest girl in the junior class," Eddie added. "I asked her out for two years straight, but she wouldn't give me the time of day. But then I joined the chess club, and she finally said she'd go out with me."

Steve found this hard to believe. Eddie didn't know a checkmate from a checkbook. "And it worked?"

"Sure. She taught me how to queen my pawn, and I taught her how to boogie till dawn."

Steve nodded. "Okay, I'll make Laura's every interest my own. What's the other thing?"

"Sacrifice," Eddie said.

"As in throw myself into the flaming crater of a volcano?" Steve asked eagerly.

"No," Eddie said. He got up to rinse his glass at the sink. "As in give up something you really love for her," he said. Then he put the glass in the dishwasher.

"That's easy! I'd give up my life for Laura," Steve said valiantly.

"Don't go overboard." Eddie opened the refrigerator door and took an apple out of the fruit bin. He tossed it up in the air, bounced it on his bicep, and then caught it. He took a big bite and continued. "But Luanne Prince really loved my favorite pale-blue V-neck sweater, so I gave it to her. She went out with me every Friday for six months after that."

"Then what happened?" Steve asked.

"Then she started liking Zachary Conrad's Vision Street Wear jacket." He shrugged, still chewing the apple. "So she switched to him. And, of course, I never got my sweater back. But like I say . . . it was worth the sacrifice."

Steve was still a little puzzled.

"But how do I know what to sacrifice?"

"Believe me," Eddie told him, "when the time comes, you'll know."

# THREE

**"SHARE THEIR INTERESTS"** had been the first half of Eddie's expert advice to Steve.

So here was Steve, the very next afternoon, taking that advice. He was attending a meeting of the Student Council. Why? Because Laura Winslow was a member. Of course, he couldn't just suddenly show up—that might make the lady suspicious. He was there in his capacity as star reporter for the school newspaper, *The Muskrat Times*. He was even dressed for the part.

"Hello, Mr. Shimata!" As Steve came in the door, he waved to the school principal. Mr. Shimata sat in on all the meetings. Steve and Mr. Shimata were old friends. Steve gave Mr. Shimata advice on how to run the school, and

Mr. Shimata gave Steve advice on how to stay out of his way. Steve took a seat in the back of the room.

*Bang*!

Student Council president Cassie Lynn Nubbles brought the gavel down on the cafeteria table and brought the meeting to order. Laura Winslow, along with four other members of the council, sat at the same table. The forty students who sat at lunch tables facing the Student Council members continued to chat among themselves.

"Quiet!" Cassie Lynn demanded, posing prettily with the gavel in her hand. From the back of the room, the flash of a camera went off. The camera belonged to Becky Sue Lohmiller, the school newspaper photographer. Becky Sue also just happened to be Cassie Lynn Nubbles's best friend. Becky Sue did everything Cassie Lynn told her to do. What more could Cassie Lynn want?

"I have an idea for this year's prom," Cassie Lynn said perkily. "I definitely think we should have one!"

Becky Sue burst into wild applause. "Oh, great idea! I love it!"

Since the school had a prom every year, everybody else in the room turned to stare at Becky Sue. When she noticed all eyes were on her, Becky Sue's smile faded. Her clapping slowed and then died out altogether. Embarrassed, she began fiddling with the light meter on her camera.

"Okay," said Cassie Lynn, beaming. "I guess that's it for new business!"

"Wait a minute, Cassie Lynn," Laura spoke up. "I'd like to raise a few issues."

At the sound of his lady love's voice, Steve jumped up and waved his pencil in the air.

"Steve Urkel, *Muskrat Times*. My avid readers would like to hear those issues, O Woman Without an Equal."

*O Slug Without an Equal*, her look told him. Lately, everywhere she was, Steve seemed to be. He had turned into her obnoxious shadow.

"We need to elect a representative to go to the next school board meeting," Laura said, addressing all the students *except* her shadow.

Cassie Lynn wrinkled her nose. "What for?"

"Well," Laura explained, "this school needs better lighting in the parking lot for security. We could also use more heat in the girls' locker room, and better facilities for the handicapped."

The students murmured in agreement.

"Oh, lighten up!" said Cassie Lynn, batting a hand at Laura. "My office needs wallpaper and a color-coordinated telephone." The Student Council president job came with an office.

Steve jumped to his feet again. "Steve Urkel, *Muskrat Times*. Question, please."

"What is it?" Cassie Lynn snapped.

"Miss Winslow here has raised some timely and powerful issues. My avid readers want to know what *you*, the Student Council president, intend to do!"

"Simple," Cassie Lynn replied with a glare. "I intend to ban you from all future meetings."

"Censorship!" Steve said, pointing a pencil at her accusingly. "I'll be writing about *that* in my next editorial."

Cassie Lynn shuffled through some papers and pretended to come across something. "Ah, here's a fun announcement! I've decided to run for another term as Student Council president. Would anyone like to nominate me?"

She looked around the room for raised hands. There was only one—Becky Sue's, of course.

"I nominate Cassie Lynn Nubbles," Becky Sue said, as if the idea had been hers.

"I second that excellent idea," said Cassie Lynn herself. "Now is there anyone idiotic enough to run against me? No? Well, okay! This meeting is…" She raised her gavel.

"Excuse me," said Mr. Shimata.

Cassie paused with the gavel in midair. "Yes, beloved Principal Shimata?" she said, batting her eyelashes.

"Cassie Lynn," he explained gently, "elections are like kissing. It's much more exciting when two people are involved."

"Oh, absolutely," Cassie agreed wholeheartedly. Then, when he wasn't looking, she rolled her eyes in disgust.

Again, Steve jumped up. "Steve Urkel, *Muskrat Times.*"

"We know!" everybody in the room shouted at once. Steve had a natural ability to grate on the nerves.

Steve went on, "I'd like to nominate someone for Student Council president. From the great state of Illinois, I nominate Laura Winslow."

"I second the nomination," said the principal.

Looking alarmed, Laura held up both hands. "Now wait a minute," she said. "I'm not sure about this."

But Mr. Shimata seemed sure. "Laura, you're bright, you're well organized, and you obviously care very much about your school," he said.

"Oh, brother!" Cassie Lynn muttered to herself.

"Personally," Mr. Shimata went on, "I think you'd make a wonderful candidate."

"Oh, yes," Steve agreed. "Yes, yes, yes!"

"Laura," Cassie Lynn said sweetly, "if you run against me, you'll get creamed."

"Oh, really?" she said, smiling into Cassie

Lynn's smug face. If Laura hadn't been interested in running before, she was now. How dare Cassie Lynn threaten her that way! "In that case, I accept the nomination!"

Steve pumped his fist high in the air. "All *right*!" Several other students cheered and clapped.

Cassie Lynn frowned. "This meeting is adjourned," she grumbled. She banged her gavel on the table.

The students filed out of the cafeteria. Steve followed Laura out into the hallway singing, "Happy days are here again."

Irritated, Laura reached back, yanked off Steve's clip-on bow tie, and stuffed it into his mouth.

While most guys wouldn't stand for this undeserved punishment, Steve welcomed it, so long as it was some form of attention from Laura. Cheerfully, he removed the tie from his mouth and bowed. "I hereby offer my humble services as your campaign manager, my dear," he said.

Laura looked at him for a long moment. How could he even *think* she might consider his offer? She shuddered at the very thought of their spending long hours together planning her strategy, making posters, and writing speeches. And the campaign would last six whole weeks!

Six weeks with Steve Urkel and she'd be more ready for a mental hospital than the Student Council.

Mr. Shimata, who just happened to have overheard Steve's offer, cleared his throat and said, "Laura, could I have a word with you alone?"

Steve watched hopefully as Mr. Shimata took Laura aside. "Now, Laura, I know you find Steve irritating."

"*Mosquitoes* are irritating, Mr. Shimata. Steve Urkel is in another league entirely."

Mr. Shimata smiled. "I don't disagree. But there's no denying that Steve is a bright boy. Remember that mock presidential election the tenth grade ran? It was Steve's team that won. And I give him complete credit for that victory. He used some very sophisticated and successful strategies."

Laura frowned and folded her arms. She hated to think that Mr. Shimata was probably right.

"What I'm trying to say is, you could do worse than choose Steve Urkel for a campaign manager," he finished.

Laura nodded. There was no denying that Steve Urkel was the smartest kid in the entire school—smarter than some of the teachers, in fact. And, even though Laura didn't make a habit of admitting it most of the time, Steve was a good friend. Plus, there was no doubt that, with his help, she would actually stand a chance against Cassie Lynn.

"Thank you for your advice, Mr. Shimata," Laura said. She took a deep breath and walked over to Steve. "Offer accepted," she said, surprised at her own decision.

Steve was no less surprised than she was. Laura's two words echoed in his ears. But then he recovered himself quickly. "Your confidence in me is appreciated. Believe me," he said, holding the door open for her, "you won't regret it."

"I hope you're right," Laura said grimly.

As soon as Steve and Laura had left the cafeteria, Becky Sue went up to Cassie Lynn. "Don't worry, Cassie Lynn," she said, "you won't lose your office and your private phone. You won't lose your gavel, either." She picked up the gavel and began polishing it on her sweater. "Laura doesn't stand a chance."

"What are you talking about?" Cassie Lynn snarled. She snatched back the gavel and pounded her open palm with it. "She's smart and she's popular!"

"You're right," Becky Sue instantly agreed. "She'll be tough to beat."

20

Cassie Lynn narrowed her eyes. "Let's not take any chances. Get some dirt on her."

Becky Sue's eyes widened. "Dirt? On Laura? She's too goody-goody."

"Oh, come on! You mean to tell me she's never cheated on a test, played hookey, or teased the football team?"

Becky Sue shook her head. "You're the only one who does those things."

Angrily, Cassie Lynn barked, "Well, don't just stand there looking stupid. Go find something on her! We've only got six weeks."

Nodding obediently, Becky backed into the table behind her and accidentally released the flash trigger on her camera. The flash exploded in Cassie Lynn's face, blinding her momentarily.

"Sorry," Becky Sue stammered. She stumbled toward the back of the room and into the hallway in search of "dirt" on Laura Winslow.

Rubbing her eyes, Cassie Lynn shook her head sadly. "Good help is *so* hard to find," she said to herself.

# FOUR

**"MY FELLOW STUDENTS,"** Laura said, "I'll never forget the day last winter when I went into the girls' locker room. My fellow students, I looked up at the window and saw a coating of ice this thick"—she held up a hand to show a gap of about an eighth of an inch between her thumb and forefinger—"on the inside of that locker room window. Ice, fellow students! Ice! So, I said to myself, Laura, this school needs heated locker rooms. With heated locker rooms, students won't get frostbite while changing into their gym clothes, or icicles that form on their wet hair after a shower.

"Now, my fellow students, if I'm elected president, I'll do my best to get heat—"

"Laura! My lovely Laura!" Steve Urkel's

annoying high-pitched voice called to her from the front steps. He was coming over to help her with the second part of her speech. He had already helped her with the first part.

"Come on in," called Laura, looking down at her speech.

Just then, the front door flew open and colored index cards, notebooks of all sizes, sharpened pencils, colored pens, rubber bands, paper clips, and erasers flew everywhere as Steve tripped on his own foot. Steve landed first, and the supplies piled on top of him. Laura just watched in amazement. How had she gotten herself into this?

Quickly, Steve got up and began to organize what he'd brought. He explained each item as he picked it up. "Blue index cards for students' rights issues, green index cards for after-school issues, yellow index cards for fund-raising issues, and pink index cards for swatting flies. I've brought twenty different colored pens for cross-referencing, five color-coded notebooks—one for notes, one for questions . . . " He went on and on until he'd explained everything down to the smallest paper clip.

He was certainly thorough. And as annoying as he could be, Laura had to admit he *was* a help. There were so many aspects to running in an election. On her own, she'd never have been aware of half of them.

"I see you've been practicing your speech, my *dear* future president," said Steve approvingly.

"I think I have it down," said Laura. "I'm ready to work on part two." She tried to ignore the *dear* as best as she could.

"Well then, get up on the coffee table and let's begin," said Steve.

"I don't know. My mom will have a fit—"

"You have to. It's like a stage. It'll prevent you from getting stage fright when reading your speech."

"Hey, Steve. Hey, Laura." Eddie came into the living room with his arm slung around Vonda Mahoney's shoulder. Vonda had made it clear to Eddie that this was *not* a date. She was *just* coming over to study. But Eddie wasn't going to let anyone else know that. "What are you doing standing on the coffee table, Laura?" he asked.

Laura looked embarrassed. "I'm practicing the speech for my first big rally," she said. "It's on Friday. Steve suggested that I stand on the coffee table. He thinks it's like a stage."

"Looks more like a coffee table to me," Eddie said.

"I'm Laura's campaign manager," Steve explained proudly. "You're just in time to hear a rousing speech from the future president of the Student Council. As you can see, we share the same interests." He winked at Eddie.

"Way to go, Urkel my man!" Eddie said, going over to Steve. They exchanged high fives. "Vonda and I share interests too. Don't we, Vonda?"

Vonda shot Eddie a suspicious look. "You mean you grow African violets too?" she asked.

"No," Eddie said. "But I surely admire them." He and Vonda headed toward the stairs. "Well, we'll be seeing y'all. Vonda and I have got some studying to do. Good luck pursuing your mutual interests."

When they were gone, Laura scowled at Steve. "What was all that business about shared interests?"

"Beats me, Sugar Beet," Steve said innocently. "Continue."

"I will," she said, "but don't call me Sugar Beet."

"I hear and I obey, my love."

"I'm not your love," Laura said through clenched teeth. Then she composed herself and looked down at her speech. "Where was I?"

"Ice," Steve said.

"Oh yeah, right....Ice, fellow students! Ice! I could actually *see* my breath in the air that day, and the—"

"Wait a minute, wait a minute, wait a minute!" Steve sprang up from the couch and held up both hands.

"What is it now?" Laura said as she looked up from her speech.

"Eye contact!" Steve said.

"What?" Laura asked, more irritated than curious.

"You have to make *eye contact* with your audience," Steve said. "You've got your *nose* in your speech when you should have your *eye* on the voter."

Laura nodded wearily. Steve probably had a point. When it came to the campaign, she was finding out that he was usually right. But that didn't make him any less annoying to have around every day.

"Okay." She sighed. "I'll start over...again."

"Pretend I'm your audience," Steve suggested, "and look deep into my eyes as you deliver your speech."

Laura groaned and rolled her eyes. This was getting to be more than she could bear.

"Lunchtime!" Harriette Winslow sang out as she bustled in from the kitchen. She carried a plate loaded with sandwiches. She stopped when she saw her daughter standing on the coffee table.

Quickly, Laura hopped down to avoid any trouble. "Sorry, Mom," she said.

Harriette set the sandwiches down on the coffee table and Steve made a dive for them.

"Mmmmm," Steve said. "Lebanese salami and

cheddar cheese. With Polish mustard. Mrs Winslow, you sure do know how to build a sandwich."

"You didn't have to do that, Mom," Laura said, admiring the plate of sandwiches. "I would have made us lunch—sooner or later."

"The last time you made lunch," her mother pointed out, "we couldn't even get your *father* to eat it. Peanut butter and mayonnaise, was it? A whimsical menu, as I recall."

Laura took a sandwich and chewed sullenly. She wished her mother hadn't brought that up. It was a day worth forgetting.

"Speaking of culinary accomplishments, Laura, my dear," Steve said, "I hear your worthy opponent, Miss Cassie Lynn Nubbles, is having a bake sale to raise campaign funds."

"So?" Laura said.

"So," Steve replied, "it wouldn't be a bad idea for us to organize a similar event. We could bake cookies, cakes, and other tasty tidbits."

"Why not have a sandwich sale instead?" Harriette suggested with a wicked grin. "Laura could whip up a batch of peanut butter and mayonnaise sandwiches—"

"And lose by a massive margin," Laura finished glumly.

"Well, I'll leave you two to your strategy. I'm going to the mall with Mother Winslow,"

Harriette said. "She wants to knit you a special campaign sweater." Harriette went back into the kitchen.

Laura and Steve sat side by side on the couch, eating their sandwiches and reading through the speech in silence.

Just then, the door opened and Richie and Judy came in. Richie was carrying Carl's new video camera.

"You'd better not let my dad see you with that," Laura said, looking up from her speech.

Richie ignored her. Then, looking disappointed, he said: "Too bad!"

"What's too bad?" Laura asked.

"We thought maybe Eddie would be in here smooching with Vonda again," Judy explained. "We wanted to record it on video tape and send it in to 'America's Yuckiest Home Videos.'"

"Maybe you two could do a little smooching for the camera instead?" Richie suggested brightly, holding the camera up to his eye.

Laura stared hard at her little cousin.

Richie shrugged. "Well, it *is* Saturday night. You usually have a date Saturday night. I mean, you two have been spending an awful lot of time together lately. Anybody might think you two were . . . you know . . . " He trailed off when he noticed Laura's vicious look.

Laura's expression changed when she realized

something. If this innocent child thought there was something going on between her and Steve, what must the kids at school be thinking?

"Don't worry, Richie," Judy said as she dragged her cousin toward the door. "They're just good friends."

# FIVE

**THE KITCHEN COUNTER** was littered with dirty pots, pans, measuring cups, and spoons. It was Sunday morning, and Laura had all day to bake. She'd woken up feeling great. Her speech was almost finished—thanks to Steve Urkel—and she felt confident about it. Flour was sprinkled everywhere. Laura held a bowl against her arm while she mixed her fourth batch of muffin batter. She held the phone between her shoulder and ear as she talked to Steve.

"Sure, Cassie Lynn Nubbles's bake sale was a success," she was saying, "but that's because she *bought* all those pies and cakes and cookies from the fanciest bakery in town. Everybody knows her father is the richest man around.... No one

30

needs to buy *me* the presidency. I can succeed on my own. I can earn money by baking blueberry muffins.... Yes, I'm baking them myself—and, get this—into each muffin I'm baking a little note that says, 'Vote for Winslow.' What do you think?...Well, of course I wrote the notes in nontoxic ink....Of course I'm warning everyone who buys a muffin that there's a message inside. I don't want people choking and suing me...."

Suddenly, she sniffed and spun around. "Smoke!" she cried. Black smoke billowed out of the oven. "My muffins are on fire!" Laura slammed down the telephone and grabbed an oven mitt. She opened the oven and choked as black smoke hit her face. She stood back helplessly as flames leaped out from the charred muffin tins.

Just then the back door burst open and Steve ran in carrying a fire extinguisher.

"Have no fear, the Urk Man is here!"

Steve stood before the oven and sprayed it with the extinguisher. In a few minutes, the oven fire was out.

He turned to Laura. "You're safe now, missy."

Laura leaned weakly against the counter, the oven mitt still on her hand. "Steve, I'm going to give you a compliment. But it's only a compliment, and it doesn't mean anything more than that."

"I understand," Steve nodded solemnly.

"You did good," she told him.

"You love me, don't you?"

"No!" Laura cried.

The two of them began to clean up the mess.

Laura and Steve were still repairing the damage when Harriette came down the back stairs a few minutes later.

"What's going on down here? Why do I smell blueberry-flavored smoke?" she wondered aloud.

"Uh," Steve said, mop in hand, "we had a little muffin mayhem. A small goof. A minor Betty Crocker boo-boo."

"Laura?" Harriette said to her daughter. "Translate."

Laura bit her lip. "I tried to bake muffins, and they came out just a weeeeee bit crispy."

Harriette examined the charred oven. Then she looked at the dial.

"Laura, this oven is set at five hundred degrees," she said.

"Well, the package said to cook at two-fifty for twenty minutes." Laura said. "I figured if I doubled the temperature I could cook them in half the time. I need to cook about a thousand of these suckers, you know."

Steve laughed and snorted. "Oh, that's rich! That's one for the books." He snorted even harder and added, "What I don't understand is how a girl so smart can do something so...so..."

Laura glared at him.

"...so...daring and adventurous!" he said, setting down the mop and heading to the door with a wave. "So long!"

As soon as he was gone, Laura turned to her mother. "Mom, I almost restarted the Chicago Fire."

"Laura, you've never shown any interest in cooking before. The closest you've come is picking up the phone to order pizza."

"Well, I decided it's time I learned how to cook. I want to be able to say I baked my own muffins for my bake sale."

"When is the bake sale?" asked Harriette.

"A week from Wednesday."

Harriette smiled. "Why don't you just say you baked them, but really let me do it?"

"But Mom, that would be dishonest."

"But altogether easier on my kitchen, don't you think?...I've got an idea," said Harriette. "The new semester starts this week. I'm sure it's not too late to sign up for home ec class. That way, you can learn the basics...in somebody else's kitchen," she added with a lopsided grin.

Laura's face lit up. "What a great idea, Mom! For two reasons. First, I'll learn how to handle myself in the kitchen, which I should learn, anyway—"

"And what's the other reason?" her mother wanted to know.

"I'll be able to get away from Steve. Home ec is one class I know he'll never take in a million years."

# SIX

**ALL DAY LONG,** Laura had been looking forward to the last period, home ec. When she finally got to that class, she was relieved to see that Steve Urkel was nowhere in sight—a first for the day! So far, Steve had been in every one of her classes. She knew she'd been right about Steve's not being the home ec type.

She looked around. There were four identical workstations, each having its own stove, sleek modern wall oven, and stainless steel sink. Surrounding each work area was a smooth, clean expanse of butcher block. She just might enjoy learning to cook in a place like this.

Suddenly, she heard a squeaking sound. It was the sound of unoiled wheels, and she would have known it anywhere. It was the sound of the wire shopping cart that Steve had been pushing around. It held his many textbooks, as well as several thick books on the subject of political strategy. These days, he never went anywhere without his campaign books. Laura's heart sank as she turned to see Steve Urkel enter the room.

Steve would now be taking every one of her classes this semester. Between school and the campaign, she'd be spending more time with him than with her own family. It didn't seem fair!

As he sat down next to her at the long wooden table, Laura turned to him in frustration. "Steve, why do you have to take every class I take?"

"Because your interests are my interests. Besides, every moment we're apart causes me deep pain."

"That's funny," she said. "I get the same pain when we're together."

Just then the bell rang, and Cassie Lynn Nubbles came in. She sat down across the table from them. *Not Cassie Lynn too*! Laura thought miserably.

"Hi, Laura," she said.

Laura's mouth opened. It was the first time since the debate earlier this week that she and Cassie had spoken.

"Hello, Cassie Lynn."

"Goodness," Cassie Lynn went on, "what a great outfit, Laura."

Laura looked down at herself. She was wearing a short bleached-denim skirt with a black and white striped polo shirt—casual but chic. She smiled her thanks.

"I love that 'thrift store' look," Cassie went on airily. "So appropriate for someone running for public office, don't you think?"

Laura's smile widened. "Why, thank you, Cassie. And I love that beauty mark. So prominent. Didn't Abe Lincoln have one just like it? Just next to his mustache?" She leaned across the table to look closer. "Oh sorry, my mistake. That's not a beauty mark—it's a big zit."

In a panic, Cassie Lynn scrounged around in her pocketbook for a mirror. Laura got up and moved over to another table, where Waldo happened to be sitting. Steve followed her, as usual.

"Waldo," Laura said, "aren't you in the wrong class? This is home ec, not drivers' ed." Waldo, in the bottom one percent of his class, usually took courses like auto repair, shop, and bicycle safety.

"Hey! I know it's home ec," Waldo said, grinning. "And I'm ready to bake, shake, whip, dip, chip, chop, and fricassee."

"You know how to cook?" Steve asked, surprised.

"Not a stitch," Waldo answered.

"Waldo, admit it," Laura said. "You're taking

home ec because you think it's a Mickey Mouse course."

"Okay," Waldo admitted, "you're onto me. I figure it's a surefire *D*. I could use at least one *D* to bring up my average."

The teacher, Ms. Steuben, had just come into the room and couldn't help but overhear Laura's and Waldo's last comments.

"I heard that, Waldo, and I want you to know this is not a Mickey Mouse course. I expect you to try your best in here, and no less."

"Okay, but I gotta warn you," Waldo said sheepishly. "My best is pretty lousy."

The bell rang to signal the start of class.

"All right, class," Ms. Steuben said, smiling, "divide yourselves up into four groups, one for each work area." Her expression changed when she saw Steve Urkel.

"You'd better get moving, Steven," Ms. Steuben said. "You'll be late for calculus."

"I'm not taking calculus this semester," Steve said. "I know more about advanced equations than the teacher does. I'm in *this* class. And I assure you, I know less about home economics than anyone else in the school. But I stand ready to master the basics."

Ms. Steuben whimpered. She had had Steve Urkel in study hall, and that had been an experience she didn't want to repeat. "That's not funny, Steven."

"Oh, I'm not joking," Steve said innocently. He laughed and snorted. But then, on a lighter note, he said, "What's cookin', good-lookin'?"

"Excuse us," Ms. Steuben said to the rest of the class. She pulled Steve off to the side of the room.

"Steve, last semester I specifically asked you what class you would *not* be taking this semester. You told me home ec. You promised," she said. There were tears of frustration in her eyes.

"Uh, yes, I did," Steve said, "but that was before I knew Laura was taking this class."

"It's not fair!" Ms. Steuben said.

"There, there, buck up. It's only a few short months." Steve patted Ms. Steuben on the back.

"Months . . . *months*?" She trembled with a look of terror on her face.

"Get a grip," Steve said.

Ms. Steuben buried her face in her hands. The thought of three months with Steve Urkel was simply too much for her to take.

# SEVEN

**LAURA'S SPEECH** had been a success—thanks to Steve Urkel. It was much better than Cassie Lynn's speech. In fact, Cassie Lynn's speech hardly covered any of the most important issues. Instead, it was filled with lots of different ways to say the same thing: elect Cassie Lynn because she's great and pretty and popular.

Laura had been so busy with the campaign that the first week of the new semester flew by. Election day was only a month away, and the bake sale was to be on the following Wednesday.

The students in home ec spent the first week learning how to bake bread—at least, most of the class learned. Others merely struggled.

Steve stood over the butcher-block counter of his workstation, happily kneading a fat lump of dough. Why shouldn't he be happy? He shared a station with his "lady love," who was standing at the counter just across from him. He hummed his favorite song, "Camptown Races," as huge billows of flour puffed out all around him.

"I'll be over tonight at seven, Laura," Steve sang out. "Will you be cooking us dinner?"

Laura glared at him through the flour all over her face. "You're coming over *after* dinner," she told him loudly. "But only to help me polish the text for my campaign flyer. Then you are going home. *H...O...M...E!*" She spoke the last line extra loudly to make sure the other students didn't get the wrong idea.

"I'll be there for dessert," Steve said, refusing to take the hint. "What'll we be having, my dear?"

Laura glared at him but then reminded herself about how much he had helped her with the campaign.

"The same thing I've served you every day this week," she said. "Blueberry muffins."

Steve's face fell. Then, reminding himself that it was for a good cause, he brightened. The bake sale was next Wednesday and Laura needed to perfect her recipe. He had to admit that Laura wasn't exactly a natural in the kitchen.

In fact, here in class she was mixing her second batch of dough. The first batch was already in the garbage can. She had mixed the wrong ingredients, using baking powder instead of yeast. Now practically everyone else was ready to put their loaves in the oven, and her dough hadn't even started rising yet.

Meanwhile, Laura noticed that Waldo, at the station across the aisle, seemed to be having as difficult a time as she was. His ingredients were spilled all over the place.

"Yech," said Cassie Lynn as she too watched, from a chair next to him. She was wearing an expensive and pretty flowered apron, and filing her nails. She did not have one bit of flour on her.

Laura wiped flour off her forehead and looked at Cassie Lynn resentfully. "Cassie Lynn, you better get on the stick and start baking your bread."

"Are you serious?" Cassie Lynn said. "I don't bake, as everybody knows. Only peasants bake their own goods."

Cassie Lynn flipped open her book bag and pulled out a loaf of store-bought white bread. She flopped it into her greased loaf pan. It fitted perfectly. "There," she said defiantly. "Bread."

Ms. Steuben came by inspecting the students' progress. "Laura, are you missing anything?" she asked.

Laura bit her lip and stared down into her bowl. "No, I don't think so," she said.

Ms. Steuben reached in and pulled a wristwatch out of the batter.

"Your watch, perhaps?"

"How about that," Laura said weakly, putting the watch to her ear. "Takes a licking and keeps on ticking."

Next Ms. Steuben looked into Cassie Lynn's pan. Then she looked at Cassie Lynn herself.

"Cassie Lynn, you could have at least taken it out of the wrapper."

"Are you saying I didn't bake this?"

"Listen up, Nubbles," Ms. Steuben said gruffly. "If you want to pass this class, you're going to have to roll up your pretty sleeves and get your hands dirty like everyone else."

Ms. Steuben slapped a ball of dough into Cassie Lynn's hands.

"Eeeeeew!" Cassie Lynn shrieked, making a face.

Ms. Steuben moved over to Waldo's workstation next. He had just pulled a roasting pan out of the oven. He lifted off the lid to reveal a golden-brown roast turkey.

"Voilà," he said.

"Waldo, what a turkey!" Ms. Steuben marveled.

Waldo looked hurt. "Hey, you don't have to like my cooking, but please don't call me names."

"No, no. I was referring to the turkey you

cooked. It looks delicious. But your assignment was to bake bread."

"I did...." He lifted up a carving knife and sharpener. With a few expert moves, he sharpened the knife, then set about carving the turkey. "But I got done early, so I made some stuffing. Then I needed something to stuff, so I got me a gobbler," he finished proudly.

Waldo laid a few slices of turkey, stuffing, and some gravy on a plate, then, with all the flourish of a master chef, presented it to Ms. Steuben.

She tasted it with her eyes closed. "Marvelous," she said, her face aglow. "It's moist and flavorful. Waldo, this is truly superior work. I'm giving you an *A*."

"Wow! Could you write that *A* on a piece of paper right now? I want to take it home and show it to my mom."

Ms. Steuben smiled warmly at him and moved on to Steve, who seemed to be in the process of talking to his bread dough.

"Rise, dough, rise! You can do it! Come on!"

"Steven," Ms. Steuben said, "having to give your food a pep talk is never a good sign."

"I don't understand," Steve said, as the kitchen timer went off. There were five minutes left before the end of class. The other students started to clean up their workstations.

Steve flung open his oven with the intention of

showing off a beautifully baked loaf of bread—
but it was far from perfect. In fact, it was flat as a
pancake.

"This can't be happening to *me*!" he exclaimed.
"I followed every single instruction!" He didn't
understand it. And it was truly humiliating that
even dim-witted Waldo could cook.

"Well, Steve," said Ms. Steuben calmly,
"baking bread can be tricky. Maybe you didn't
knead it long enough, or maybe you didn't
measure correctly. Or you might have opened the
oven too soon. Lots of things can go wrong.
Look, at least you tried as hard as you could.
That's why I'll be generous and give you a *C*."

Steve stiffened with shock. "A what? A *what*?"
In his entire school career, he had never gotten
anything lower than an *A*, on anything, at any
time, anywhere.

"A *C*," Ms. Steuben repeated mildly. "A *C*."

"But I've never...gotten less than an *A*!"

"So?"

"So, I can't live with a *C*. It'll ruin my record."

"Steven, get hold of yourself."

"I can't. The room is spinning. I'm dizzy. Oh,
my Lord, I feel *stupid*!"

Ms. Steuben grabbed him by the shoulders and
shook him good and hard until finally he came to
his senses.

"Steven," she said, "it's not too late to transfer

to another class, you know."

Steve thought about it for a moment, then shook his head. "No, I need to be near Laura."

Ms. Steuben raised an eyebrow. "Is being near Laura so important that you could stand to get straight *C*'s all semester long?"

Steve nodded firmly, feeling a little sick inside.

"All right, Steven, suit yourself."

Steve shuddered at the thought of getting straight *C*'s. Feeling weak in the knees, he sank into the nearest chair.

"Well, Eddo," he said to the air, imagining the face of his friend and onetime adviser. "Here I thought I was only sharing interests with my lady love, but it looks like I'll be sacrificing something I love while I'm at it—my beloved grade average. Did you hear that, Laura? I'm sacrificing my beautiful straight-*A* average for you, my love!" He looked around for Laura, but the home ec room was silent and empty. Laura, the other kids, and Ms. Steuben had gone, leaving Steve alone with his dead bread dough and his *C*.

# EIGHT

**EDDIE, JUDY, AND RICHIE** came piling down the back stairs into the kitchen. Laura dragged down last.

"I want bacon and eggs," Eddie said.

"Make mine waffles," Judy said.

"I'll take ice cream," little Richie piped up.

"Guess what?" Harriette said, in response to their requests. "You're all eating muffins."

Laura's bake sale the day before had been a fabulous success. And once again, Steve Urkel had helped to make it that way. He had gotten Waldo to help her out with the baking—after all, Waldo *was* this year's number-one home ec student, wasn't he?

Laura had sold 500 muffins at a quarter apiece. The only problem was that 750 had been baked—and many of the remaining 250 were still in the Winslow kitchen.

Only Richie seemed enthusiastic. He tore into his blueberry muffin and lifted out the slip of paper.

"What does your fortune say, Judy?"

Judy gave her little cousin a pitying look. "They all say the same thing, brainiac: 'Vote for Winslow.'"

Richie wrinkled his nose. "What kind of fortune is that?" he wanted to know.

"It's your cousin Laura's fortune," Rachel said, as she buttered her muffin and ate it with a hot cup of coffee.

Laura, who had vowed never to eat another blueberry muffin as long as she lived, was eating cereal this morning. She had just poured milk into her bowl when Steve Urkel, wearing a plumed velvet hat, came through the back door. "'But, soft! what light through yonder window breaks? It is the east, and' *Laura* 'is the sun.'"

Everyone looked up from their breakfasts.

"I know that speech!" Judy said. "That's from William Shakespeare's *Romeo and Juliet*."

"That's right, Judy, very good," Steve said.

Richie turned to his cousin. "How did you know?"

"Unlike you," she answered, "I read *more* than comic books and cereal boxes."

"Why would you want to do that?" Richie said.

Judy rolled her eyes.

"The word is out, Laura," Steve said, "that later this week you'll be auditioning for the first drama class play of the semester—for none other than the part of Juliet. I just wanted you to know that I too will be involved in the play, because, as you know, your interests are my interests." He secretly winked at Eddie, who gave him the thumbs-up sign.

Laura didn't exactly jump up and down with enthusiasm. She let her cereal spoon plop into her bowl. She had suddenly lost her appetite.

"My granddaughter Laura, starring as Juliet?" Mother Winslow said. "I think that's wonderful!"

Laura nodded. "Yeah, well I haven't gotten the part yet, Grandma."

"But you will, my love," Steve said. "Who better to star in the Bard's immortal tragedy of two . . ."—he crossed the room, leaned over, and whispered the rest into her ear—"star-crossed lovers?" He straightened and said aloud, "Doesn't that give you the shivers, my sweet?"

"Well, my skin is definitely crawling," Laura said.

"Steve," Mother Winslow said, "why don't you try out for the part of Romeo?"

Laura nearly choked.

It was Eddie who answered first. "I don't think so, Grandma," he said, laughing. "That would make it a comedy . . . no, science fiction . . . no, come to think of it, it *would* be a tragedy after all."

"Regrettably," Steve said, "those exact words were uttered by Ms. Mooney, the drama teacher. She was bright enough to see that my dashing good looks and remarkable physical abilities would overshadow the rest of the cast."

"So she made you stage manager?" Laura guessed.

Steve nodded glumly. "Yeah, that's right."

Laura breathed a sigh of relief and picked up her spoon. Now that she knew Steve would not be Romeo, her appetite had suddenly returned.

Steve spun around and made his way back to the door. Before leaving, he swept the plumed hat off his head and bowed gallantly to Laura. " 'Good night, good night! parting is such sweet sorrow, that I shall say good night till it be morrow.' "

He spun dramatically and walked smack into the wall next to the door. With an embarrassed *snort, snort* and a laugh, Romeo Urkel rubbed his sore nose and went out the door—the right way this time.

Laura turned back to her cereal. "I'm so tired of him just barging in," she said to no one in particular. "We've got to save up for a moat."

"I don't know how you can speak of the boy in such a way," Mother Winslow said. "He's had so many clever ideas for your campaign. Those radio spots he managed to place. The posters in all the local stores. And the skywriter writing 'Winslow! Woweee!' above Chicago. Now that was truly a brilliant idea. I was never so proud."

Rachel was as interested in the campaign as any of the Winslows. She had even named the blueberry sundae at Rachel's Place the "Laurapalooza," in honor of her niece's candidacy. But show business interested her far more than politics, and she had always secretly thought that Laura had star quality.

"You're really trying out for Juliet?" she asked, her eyes shining.

"Of course she isn't," Carl said, entering the kitchen with his video camera. "She can't act in a play and run for office. Not even my well-rounded daughter could do that."

"Don't be so sure," Harriette said. "My own mother always used to say, 'The more you do, the more you can do.'" She noticed Carl filming her. "Hey, put that down!" she said.

"I want to make a family breakfast video," Carl said. "Now if I lean it up against this vase, I can be in it too." He fiddled with some buttons, placed the camera on the table, and squeezed in between Judy and Richie, who were each on their second muffin.

Laura put her hand over the camera. "This is serious. What should I do? The election is in about four weeks. The play is in three weeks. They cast it this week and then go into two weeks of intensive rehearsal. I don't know . . . it might be hard going for a couple of weeks there, handling both . . . but I think I'd like to try."

Carl reached for the video camera, turned it off, and sat down at the table. He realized it wasn't the time for pictures. Laura's decision was more important.

"It can't hurt to audition, honey," said Harriette. "You'd be great."

"Absolutely," Rachel agreed. "After all, you're related to *me*, and I'm a wonderful actress."

"That's true," Harriette said, hiding a smile. "Why, I've seen you tell a man you're twenty-three without even blinking."

Rachel frowned and put her hands on her hips. "Excuse me, oh humorous one, but have you forgotten that when we did *The Wizard of Oz* in sixth grade, they made *me* the Wicked Witch of the East?"

"Which witch was that?" Mother Winslow wanted to know.

"The one that the house fell on," Rachel said.

"But I got applause when I curled up my feet and went 'Ooof.' "

"They were just happy you were dead," Harriette said, smirking.

Suddenly, an odd beeping noise filled the kitchen. Everybody looked around.

"What's that?" Mother Winslow said. "A fire alarm?"

"It's my new phone pager," Carl said, rising to go to the phone. "Lieutenant Murtagh has given one to each of his key men, so he knows where to reach us in case of emergency. You know, terrorist attacks, bank robberies, stuff like that," he said as he dialed headquarters.

"Sergeant Winslow responding to the page," he said into the receiver.

The others watched Carl as he listened to the voice at the other end of the line. He nodded solemnly and said, "Will do, sir. Immediately, sir. Over and out." Gravely, he hung up the phone.

"What is it, dear?" Harriette sounded worried.

"I've got to leave immediately," Carl said. "I've got an important mission to carry out."

Harriette frowned. "What mission is that, dear?"

Carl looked a little embarrassed. "I . . . uh . . . promised Lieutenant Murtagh I'd pick up his uniform at the dry cleaners."

Harriette shook her head, partly in relief, partly in disgust that her husband would let his boss take such unfair advantage of him. But all she did was sigh and kiss Carl good-bye.

Rachel leaned over toward Laura. "Check out this performance," she whispered, flinging out her arms theatrically. "Carl, don't go out there alone! We love you, you big, crazy lug." She jumped up and ran to the door, which had closed behind Carl. "When will it all end? The robbing, the killing, the uniform picking-upping . . . I just can't take it anymore!"

Dramatically, she swept her forehead with the back of her hand as if she were going to faint. Then she lowered her arms and, in a normal voice, said, "You know, I've still got it."

"Yeah," her sister said dryly. "But who *wants* it?"

Judy and Richie giggled as they finished their muffins.

# NINE

**LAURA WAS SITTING** on a metal folding chair on the stage. As she waited to audition for the part of Juliet, she felt confident. Aunt Rachel had helped her memorize a section of Juliet's lines over the weekend, and promised to help her rehearse the part if she won it.

"You're on next," Ms. Mooney told her.

Laura took a deep breath and went over in her mind what Rachel had taught her. In a few seconds, she had succeeded in transporting herself to the garden of the Capulets.

"All right, Laura . . ."—Ms. Mooney's voice pierced her nearly trancelike state—"you're on."

She opened her eyes and stood up. As fair Juliet of Verona, she walked gracefully to center stage.

" 'O Romeo, Romeo! wherefore art thou Romeo? . . .' "

She went through her lines without a single mistake. When she finished the reading, she felt she had done well. And the look in Ms. Mooney's eyes confirmed this.

She returned to her seat, satisfied. Maxine, her best friend, who had already tried out for the Juliet part a few minutes earlier, squeezed Laura's hand hard. "You were great!" she whispered, her eyes sparkling. "How did you get to be so good?"

"Practice," Laura whispered back.

It was true—she had worked hard all week. Even if she didn't get the part, the audition would have been worth it. Preparing had taken up so much time that she had left the campaigning to Steve. His job as stage manager left him with a lot of free time.

Laura and Maxine settled down to watch the rest of the auditions. A girl named Cyndy read for the part of Juliet's nurse. Another girl, named Rebecca, read for Juliet. Two boys read for the part of Mercutio.

Finally, the auditions came to an end. Ms. Mooney crossed to center stage. She was followed by Steve, who carried a bull horn he had borrowed from Carl.

"Thank you, everyone, for coming today," Ms. Mooney said.

Steve spoke into the bull horn: "THANK

YOU, EVERYONE, FOR COMING TODAY!"

Cringing, Ms. Mooney covered her ears, then went on. "You were all very good . . ."

"YOU WERE ALL VERY GOOD . . . ," Steve echoed.

"Stop that," Ms. Mooney said, turning to Steve.

"STOP THAT," Steve repeated.

"Now!" she said.

"NOW!"

Ms. Mooney grabbed away the bull horn and said, with strained patience, "Take a seat, Steven."

"Where?" Steve asked cheerfully.

"Pittsburgh," she said through clenched teeth.

Steve let out with a *laugh, laugh, snort.* "Ms. Mooney, you tickle me."

Ms. Mooney smiled faintly and turned back to the group. "As I was saying . . . your auditions were excellent. I have decided that the part of Romeo will be played by Daniel Wallace."

The kids applauded. Daniel Wallace, a tall and handsome kid, rose and took a bow.

Maxine nudged Laura and whispered, "I knew he'd get it. He's gorgeous."

"Yeah," Laura agreed. "I can't wait to see him in tights." The girls stamped their feet and squealed into the palms of their hands.

Ms. Mooney continued. "I've narrowed the

choices for Juliet down to two girls. It will be either . . . Maxine or Laura."

Laura and Maxine sat bolt upright, eyes wide.

"Daniel, will you please read with the ladies?" Ms. Mooney said.

Daniel smiled, showing two perfectly straight rows of dazzling white teeth. "It will be my pleasure."

Again, Laura and Maxine squealed into their hands. Watching them, Steve shook his head in disgust. He hated to see Laura act this way—crazy for another guy.

"Maxine," Ms. Mooney said, "you read first."

But Maxine was still too shocked to move. Seeing this, Daniel went over and offered her a hand. Trembling, Maxine took his hand, rose from her chair, and followed him, zombielike, to center stage. Steve handed them the pages they were supposed to read. Then he stood back and cued Daniel to begin.

Daniel nodded. He read his lines and then waited for Maxine to respond. But Maxine just stood there staring at him and sighing dreamily, not saying a word.

" 'O! speak again, bright angel,' " Daniel said, covering for her.

With a dopey smile, Maxine spoke. "You are *so* gorgeous!"

The other kids giggled. It was the truth, but it wasn't Shakespeare.

Ms. Mooney cleared her throat. "Thank you, Maxine. Interesting interpretation."

Maxine floated back to her seat, apparently unaware that she had blown it.

"How'd I do?" she asked Laura.

Laura grinned. "You were great."

"Laura," Ms. Mooney said, "It's your turn. Let's start with line thirty-one, Act Two, Scene Two."

Laura got up and joined Daniel. She ignored the pages Steve held out to her. She didn't need them—she knew the lines by heart. It was her favorite scene ("O gentle Romeo! If thou dost love, pronounce it faithfully . . ."). While they recited their lines, the other kids watched in hushed admiration. Laura and Daniel *were* Romeo and Juliet.

"There's our Juliet," Ms. Mooney whispered to Steve.

"You said a mouthful," Steve said, staring at Laura. His eyes were soft with adoration.

Laura and Daniel moved closer to each other, totally caught up in their roles.

" 'Good night, good night!' " continued Laura, " 'parting is such sweet sorrow, that I shall say good night till it be morrow.' "

They kissed. Everybody sighed. It was truly a romantic moment—to everybody but Steve, that is.

As far as Steve was concerned, this kiss was now on overtime—it had gone on long enough. He waved his arms trying to get their attention, but they ignored him and continued to kiss. He began to jump up and down and clap his hands, signaling that the scene was over—*finito*—and the kiss was over too.

Finally, in desperation, he snatched the bull horn from Ms. Mooney and bellowed into it: "CUT! CUT!"

But the kiss went on.

"I SAID *CUT*, FOR CRYING OUT LOUD!" Steve shouted.

At last, Laura and Daniel broke apart, but they continued to stare into each other's eyes as Steve looked on, feeling helpless, feeling left out, feeling like a total chump. Now he was going to have to stand by for two weeks of watching Laura smooching with another guy. This wasn't part of his plan. This wasn't supposed to happen. His Juliet wasn't supposed to wind up in the arms of any Romeo but himself.

# TEN

**LAURA AND RACHEL** were in the living room practicing Laura's lines. The first week of rehearsals had flown by. There was only one more week to go until the performance and then another week before the Student Council election. Laura looked forward to the end of her aunt's coaching. It was beginning to irritate her.

"Always remember," Rachel was saying, "that great acting comes from within. Legendary performances come from actors who reach deep down into their souls and dredge up *pain*. . . . Do you feel it, Laura? Do you feel a pain?"

Laura turned to her aunt. "I feel a pain," she said, "and I'm hoping she will go tuck her son in."

Rachel was as bad about the play as Steve was

about the campaign—always at it. Didn't either of them have a life of their own?

Carl came hurrying down the stairs. He'd gotten an emergency beep from Lieutenant Murtagh.

"Where are you going, Dad?" Laura asked.

"I have to go pick up a burger and fries for Murtagh. He hasn't eaten since breakfast." He sounded miserable. "You know, I don't think this night can get any worse." He opened the front door to the sight of a grinning Steve Urkel.

"Hi-dee-ho, Winslows!" Steve sang out.

"I was wrong," Carl said dully. "It just got worse." And he trudged off to do his errands.

"Laura!" Steve said eagerly. "Awful, bad, terrible news."

"What?" Laura asked suspiciously. He didn't look like the carrier of bad news—he looked happy.

"Daniel Wallace is in the hospital with appendicitis."

The script Laura was holding dropped from her hands and slid to the floor. "But we open in one week! Who's gonna play Romeo?"

Steve grinned broadly.

Laura's jaw dropped. "Oh, no."

Steve's grin widened. All during the week's rehearsals he had stood in the wings memorizing Romeo's lines—just in case of an emergency. And now, thanks to fate, the emergency had arrived. Ms. Mooney had no choice but to appoint Steve as Daniel's replacement. After all, Steve was the only one who knew Romeo's lines by heart. Steve felt a surge of joy. Now, Laura really was going to be his Juliet.

Laura didn't share the joy. Far from it! She backed away from him. "No, please!"

Steve followed and went down on one knee before her. "Yes, my cuddly Capulet. When we perform the famous balcony scene, it'll be my lips pressed hotly against yours."

Laura grimaced and turned to her aunt.

"Aunt Rachel?" she said faintly.

"Yes, Laura."

"That pain you were talking about?" she said, looking as if she were about to be sick. "Now I've really found it."

# ELEVEN

***CLICK. CLICK. WHRRRRR.***

Carl sat in the audience with his video camera aimed at the stage. This was a proud night for Carl, watching his daughter star in one of the great plays of all time.

As the curtain rang down on the first act, he jumped to his feet and hollered, "Bravo! Bravo, Juliet!"

"Carl, sit down," Harriette said, tugging at his jacket.

But Carl was going to do no such thing. He bounded out into the aisle and continued to applaud. "How 'bout that Juliet!" he said to the rest of the audience.

It took Rachel, Eddie, and Mother Winslow to drag him back to his seat and get him settled.

"Poor Laura," Rachel said, sighing.

"What do you mean?" Harriette asked.

"The balcony scene is next," said Rachel. "The 'kiss' scene. Think she'll really kiss Steve?" During their home rehearsals, there hadn't been an exercise to prepare Laura for the moment to come.

Just then, the lights dimmed. The audience grew quiet and settled in once again.

"Shhh," said Rachel. "Here we go—the balcony scene."

Eddie nudged Richie and whispered, "Five bucks says she doesn't kiss him."

Richie shook his head. "Forget it," he said. "I'm not interested in losing money."

The curtain opened on the Capulet orchard. A large artificial tree stood before Juliet's balcony. Other smaller trees stood nearby. Hanging from a string overhead was a cardboard crescent moon. Harp and flute music played over the speaker system.

Even costumed in gray tights and a green velvet jacket, Steve managed to pull off the classic high-waisted Urkel Look—especially when he tugged up his tights as he walked.

With a last tug, Steve looked up at Laura, who had just stepped out onto her balcony.

"'But, soft! what light through yonder window breaks?'" Steve began.

Laura looked out from the balcony, resting her cheek on her hand, fully focused on Steve. When it came time for her to speak, she said: "'Ay me!'" and sighed.

From the audience came a loud: "Bravo! That's my baby!" Carl hadn't been able to hold himself back.

Steve broke out of character long enough to shoot Carl a disapproving look. At the same time, Harriette gave Carl a sharp elbow to the ribs. *That* shut him up.

Back in character, Steve said, "'She speaks: O! speak again, bright angel . . .'"

"'O Romeo, Romeo! Wherefore art thou Romeo? . . .'" Laura recited, after a few more lines from Steve.

Steve couldn't believe how smoothly everything was going—until he had to climb the big tree near the balcony. *That* didn't go too smoothly. After all, he had had only a week to rehearse, and he wasn't the athletic type.

"'Dost thou love me? . . .'" Laura's Juliet asked. "'O gentle Romeo! if thou dost love, pronounce it faithfully . . .'"

Steve crawled out onto the branch that was nearest the balcony. As suavely as he could, he swung from the branch over to Laura. Graceful he wasn't. But at least he landed on the balcony, with a loud thump—on both bony knees.

Several people in the audience giggled.

"Oucheth!" Steve said, trying his best to keep in Romeo character.

Laura helped him to his feet. "Steve, are you okay?" she asked under her breath.

Steve winced, rubbed his knees, and whispered back, "I think I bent my dagger." But it wasn't the time to worry about the dagger. The show had to go on. Steve pulled down his jacket, tugged up his tights, and waited for his lady love's next line.

Both Steve and Laura felt their hearts pounding. As they were both only too aware, the scene with the kiss was fast approaching. It was a scene Laura dreaded, and one Steve had spent his entire life longing for.

"'Good night, good night! . . .'" With dread in her heart, Laura found herself reciting the lines that would end in the kiss.

Steve turned and spritzed his mouth quickly with breath freshener. Then he turned back to Laura and prepared his lips for the one, the only . . . the kiss!

"'. . . parting is such sweet sorrow, that I shall say good night till it be morrow.'" Laura paused, clenched her fists, and thought, *Oh God, I wish it were morrow.*

Steve stood there with his lips puckered. Laura summoned up her courage and then gave him a quick peck on the lips.

Steve's eyes flew open. "Zowie!" he cried. "Yowie! Whoaaaaa, Mama!"

He lifted his dagger and swept it through the air in triumph over the kiss. What happened next was hard, if not impossible, to follow.

The dagger accidentally cut one of the two strings holding up the moon. The moon, dangling now from only one string, began to fly upward, bringing the curtain with it. As the moon disappeared, a bag of sand came crashing downward.

Steve and Laura ducked as the bag swung across the stage like a wrecking ball. It smashed into the house, and the balcony railing collapsed. The entire front of the balcony fell off and took the tree with it, crashing to the floor. Four other sandbags fell down from above, destroying the entire Capulet orchard and every last bit of scenery on the stage.

Standing in the middle of the wreckage, Steve looked out at the audience with one hand to his mouth. "Didst I do that?" he asked innocently.

# TWELVE

"GET... OUT... OF... here!" Laura screamed. With each word, she flung something new at Steve—a script, a bouquet of flowers her father had given her after the play, the vase she had put them in, a cold piece of pizza left over from the dress rehearsal.

Steve stood in the doorway of the girls' dressing room and ducked as each item sailed over his head.

He had stood in the hall for fifteen minutes waiting patiently while the Winslows all crowded around Laura. They had come backstage to congratulate Laura on the wonderful job she had done—even though everything had come undone about halfway through the play.

And now it was his turn, but of course congratulations weren't uppermost in his mind. He wanted to tell her how sorry he was for ruining her special night. But she didn't seem to want to hear it. He had seen Laura mad, but never this mad. She was furious!

The other cast members had left for the cast party, but Laura was in no mood to celebrate. Steve was relieved to have this time alone with her, but he had to wait until there was nothing left to throw before he could speak. "Won't you even let me apologize?" he said.

Laura had changed out of her costume into a T-shirt and jeans. But she looked better than ever to Steve.

"Apologize. APOLOGIZE?" Laura's voice rose. "You actually think that a mere *apology* will make up for what you did this evening. You took a beautiful, wonderful play and turned it into a . . . a . . . farce!"

Actually, the audience had liked what Steve had done. They had given the actors a standing ovation and five curtain calls. They loved it so much they hadn't let the cast finish the play. But Laura had not liked it at all. While the cast members were cleaning up the stage, Laura hadn't said a word to Steve. In fact, she couldn't even bring herself to look at him.

"You're right," Steve said. "I'm a jerk. I ruined the play."

"You certainly did," Laura said. She tossed her makeup into her overnight case.

"And I'm sorry . . . from the bottom of my heart, I'm sorry," Steve went on softly. "And I hope you'll find it in your heart to forgive me. Maybe not tonight, maybe not even tomorrow, but someday."

She was silent. Steve, taking her silence as encouragement, began on a brighter note. "Besides, it's important that you put this behind you and concentrate on the election. Our voters go to the polls next week. I'm sure I don't need to remind you of that. And I want to take this opportunity to say what an honor it has been, serving as your campaign manager—"

"And that's another thing." She turned on him fiercely. "I'm tired of looking at your face. Everywhere I've turned, for the past five weeks, I've seen Steve Urkel. First, you take over my campaign. Then you're in every class I'm taking this semester. Now you take over my play. You're over every night playing politics. You're smothering me, Steve—smothering me! I can't stand it. I need to breathe."

Steve looked hurt. "I...I'm sorry. I didn't realize..." He swallowed and backed away slowly. "I guess this means you don't want my help."

For one wild moment, Laura actually thought

of firing him as her manager. But she knew she couldn't do that. Without him, her campaign would be rudderless.

"No, Steve," she said reluctantly. "I still do need your help. I just need...a little breathing room, that's all."

Steve couldn't hide his smile. He was still her manager! She hadn't fired him!

"Absolutely! I'll give you lots of breathing room," he told her. "I'll see you in school on Monday. I've had the volunteers working all this week on one last round of posters—to remind the voters to vote next Friday. Oh, Laura, I know you can win this. I know it!"

And, with his battered hopes on the mend once again, Steve left his Juliet. And Laura now turned her still-gloomy thoughts to cleaning up the mess she had made.

# THIRTEEN

**LAURA AND STEVE** spent lunch hour on the last Tuesday before Friday's election going around the school replacing posters that had fallen down, and mending those that had been ripped or otherwise defaced.

"It's important that we keep our image fresh right up until the last minute," Steve had lectured her.

He looked up at one poster and read the slogan aloud. "'Winslow! Wow!' My sentiments, exactly."

But "Winslow! Wow!" had a big rip down the middle.

Steve carried a small stepladder. Laura carried the posters and tape. Since he was already carrying the ladder, it was Steve's job to set it up and hold it steady while Laura climbed it and mended the posters with tape.

Steve set up the ladder, whipped out his handkerchief, and began to dust off the ladder rungs for Laura. He was happy to see that her attitude toward him had, over the weekend, subsided from red-hot fury to mild frost.

Laura climbed up to the second rung. As she was reaching to tape the rip in the poster, a boy walked by. He took one look at her legs and let out a wolf whistle.

"Hey! What are you, some sort of sleazoid!" Steve said with a disapproving frown. He shooed the boy off with his hankie.

At the other end of the hall, Cassie Lynn paused to admire one of her own posters before opening her locker.

"'End your troubles with Cassie Lynn Nubbles!'" she read the slogan aloud. "What a candidate!"

The campaign had cost her father hundreds of dollars in catering fees, professional photographers, and a new wardrobe for his daughter. For a while, she was really afraid she was going to lose. She hated the thought of losing the private office and the telephone. But then Laura had gotten involved in the play and left Urkel to do her campaigning. It was just the edge Cassie

Lynn needed. Dreaming of victory, Cassie opened her locker.

She had decorated the inside of the locker in a costly gold metallic wallpaper. The shelves were lined with scented, cushioned pink satin. She pulled out a lighted makeup mirror and applied her lipstick. As she was standing back and admiring herself in the mirror, Becky Sue came up behind her.

"Hi, Cassie Lynn," she said. "I love that color."

"I hate it." Cassie Lynn tossed the lipstick into her locker temperamentally.

"Me too," Becky Sue quickly agreed.

"So..." Cassie Lynn fluffed her hair and turned away from the mirror. "Have you bought me any more votes today?"

Meanwhile, Steve and Laura had been working their way down the hall toward Cassie's locker, where one of Laura's posters had come unstuck in one corner. Steve set up the ladder nearby and again dusted off the rungs with his hankie.

"Okay. Do your stuff, Lovepuff." The name was out of his mouth before he could stop it.

"Forgive me, Light of My Life...I mean, dearest...I mean, Ms. Winslow."

She gave him a dirty look and climbed up. The lockers were taller here so she had to stand on the topmost rung to reach the wall above them.

Just then, she turned quickly and lost her balance. She toppled over backward, her arms waving wildly in the air. Panicking, Steve—Mr. Uncoordinated himself—managed to hold out both arms and, to his extreme surprise, catch her. They looked, for that fleeting instant, like they were locked in a romantic embrace. Laura hoped no one had seen her fall, but she was out of luck.

"Don't just stand there—take their picture!" Cassie Lynn whispered to Becky Sue. They had seen the whole thing. This was the opportunity Cassie Lynn had been waiting for the entire campaign!

Becky Sue removed her camera from its case and took a picture. *Click! Click! Click!* She took three more.

"You know," Steve said to Laura in a dreamy voice, "I could hold you like this forever." The flashes from the camera made him think he was seeing heavenly stars.

"You've got one more second," Laura said between her teeth.

Very, very slowly, Steve began to count. "One, Mississippi, two…"

"Time's up!" Laura said. Very reluctantly, he released her. He felt a little dazed.

Cassie Lynn and Becky Sue came down the hall toward them.

"Look, Becky Sue," Cassie Lynn said, her

voice oozing with phony sympathy. "Poor Laura has worked so hard all these weeks! And now she's going to have to drop out of the race."

"Yes, it's so sad," Becky Sue agreed woefully.

Laura looked puzzled. "What are you talking about?"

"We just took some very hot photos of you being romanced by the Prince of Passion here," Cassie said.

"What?" Steve blurted out. "She just slipped and I caught her, that's all."

"Becky Sue," Cassie Lynn said to her friend, "we should put these pictures in the school paper. We're just in time to make this week's edition."

"Oh, we couldn't do that," Becky Sue said sarcastically. "Everyone would think that Laura is in love with Steve Urkel and no one would vote for her!"

"I told you, she just slipped," Steve said with mounting irritation.

"That might be what happened, but it won't be what people will believe." Cassie rubbed her palms together gleefully. "They love juicy gossip."

"You wouldn't dare!" Laura said, eyes narrowed and hands on hips. The world would think she and Steve were an item—this was her worst nightmare come true!

"Try me." Cassie smiled. It wasn't a nice smile.

"You've got twenty-four hours to drop out of the race or we publish these pictures." Cassie Lynn and Becky Sue turned on their heels and walked down the hall.

Sputtering mad, Steve started to chase after them. "Come back here, you . . . you hussy!" he shouted.

But Laura simply reached out and grabbed the back of Steve's shirt. "Steve . . . ," she said, holding him back.

"Come back here!" Steve continued after the girls. But now his feet slipped on the floor and his arms flailed.

"Steve . . . ," Laura repeated.

He finally stopped waving his arms and turned around to Laura, who still had a handful of his shirt. "What?"

"Never mind about them!" she said.

"Never mind?" Steve balled up his fists. "That cheap, lowdown, underhanded, bushwacking, mudslinging, slanderous snake in a skirt is blackmailing you!"

"I know," Laura said. She leaned against the locker and slid down until she was sitting on the floor. There she cradled her chin in her hands. Suddenly, she felt very, very tired.

"Aren't you going to fight her?" Steve asked.

Laura shook her head. "I give up," she said.

"Give up?" Steve said. "You can't give up! Think of all the work we've done."

"Exactly. And the fact that she can undo all that hard work with one nasty little trick makes me so depressed I just don't think I want to go on."

"Don't say that," Steve said. He reached down and, grabbing Laura by the shoulders, pulled her to her feet. "I won't let you give up. You owe it to your fellow students to see this through to the end, and I'm going to make sure you do even if I have to . . . " He trailed off, already thinking of a plan.

"Have to what?" Laura asked, curious in spite of herself. She didn't want to have to drop out of the race if she could help it. Could he really help her? She dared to hope.

"Never mind, Madam President. I'll handle it. Trust me."

# FOURTEEN

**THE NEXT DAY** between classes, Cassie Lynn Nubbles stood in the hallway campaigning. Her right hand was free to shake hands. In her left hand she held a medium-size wicker basket.

She delivered her slogan to all who would listen: "Vote for Nubbles; wave bye-bye to troubles." She saw a girl she knew. "Carol," she said, "will you vote for me?"

Carol shrugged. "I'm not sure."

Cassie Lynn reached into the wicker basket. "Here, have a locker sachet. I'm rich. Now will you vote for me?"

Carol took the sachet, which smelled like lavender. "Sure!" she said eagerly.

From a classroom doorway nearby, Steve and

Eddie had been watching Cassie in action. "There's one crooked politician for you," Steve said, shaking his head sadly.

"Well, it's up to us to straighten her out," Eddie said.

"Ready, Eddo?" Steve turned to Laura's older brother.

At dinner last night, Eddie Winslow had noticed how miserable his sister Laura was. He had never seen her so upset before—and it was all because of this Cassie Lynn Nubbles person. He squared his shoulders and nodded firmly. "I'm psyched. Let's do it."

Together, they came up behind Cassie Lynn. Steve tapped her on the shoulder. She turned and sneered when she saw who it was.

"Nubs," Steve said, "a moment of your time, if you please."

"Nubs?" Cassie Lynn cried out, outraged at the nickname.

"You and I have some unfinished business to take care of, Nubsarino," Steve informed her.

Before Cassie Lynn could react to the name, the bell rang. "Later, nerd child," she said. "I've got to get to class." She started over to her locker to stow the basket, but Steve and Eddie followed her.

Steve tapped Cassie Lynn on the shoulder.

"This will only take a second," he said. "Do you still intend to publish that picture of Laura and me if she doesn't drop out of the election?"

"I most certainly do."

"Is there any way I can talk you out of it?" Steve said.

"Well, let me think . . . no," she said almost immediately.

"Are you aware that what you are doing is morally wrong?" Steve asked.

"Well, sure! But you know what they say: all's fair in love and politics."

Steve grinned. "I'm glad you said that."

With that, Steve put his arms around Cassie and planted a big kiss on her lips.

Kissing Cassie Lynn Nubbles was, for Steve Urkel, the ultimate sacrifice. But he had thought long and hard about it, and it was the only way to save Laura's honor.

According to plan, Eddie whipped out a camera from his backpack, stepped back quickly, and began snapping pictures. *Click! Click! Click!* When Eddie had snapped half a dozen photos of Steve Urkel romancing Cassie Lynn Nubbles, Steve released her and stood back.

Cassie Lynn wiped her mouth on her sweater sleeve. "*Ptooie! Ptooie! Ptooie! Yuck! Ecch!*"

"Hey," Steve said, insulted. "The earth didn't exactly move for me, either."

Cassie Lynn stared at him in horror. "Are you out of your geeky mind?"

"I don't think so," Steve said calmly. "Why, I can see the headline now... 'Nubbles Sucks Face with Nerd!'"

Cassie Lynn's jaw dropped. "You wouldn't!" she gasped.

"Would."

"You couldn't!"

"Could."

"But it's a lie! You kissed *me*, I didn't kiss you."

"That may be what happened, but it won't be what people believe. People love juicy gossip." Steve gloated as he repeated to her her very own words.

"Well, I refuse to drop out of the race," Cassie Lynn snapped.

"I don't want you to," Steve said. "All I want is a fair election. If you don't publish your picture, I won't publish mine."

"You want the students to decide between Laura and me for themselves?" Cassie Lynn said, as if she found the idea truly a hideous one.

"It's an idea that might be just crazy enough to work!" Steve said.

"It's a deal," Cassie Lynn said, shoving the basket of sachets in her locker. "I'm going to gargle with Lysol." She slammed her locker shut and stormed off.

"It worked!" Steve said. He slapped Eddie with a high five.

"Way to go, Steve," Eddie said, satisfied. He didn't want a picture of his sister in Steve Urkel's arms in the school newspaper—even if Steve wasn't such a bad guy.

"She's not so smart after all," Steve said.

"I'll say." Eddie stared at the camera. "If she was *really* smart, she'd have noticed that I forgot to take the lens cap off."

Steve threw back his head and laughed the Urkel laugh: *snort, snort, snicker, snicker*!

# FIFTEEN

**FRIDAY FINALLY ARRIVED**. It had
been the longest week of Laura Winslow's life.
The crucial twenty-four-hour period had passed
without Cassie Lynn Nubbles putting Operation
Blackmail into effect. But Laura had still felt the
threat. Every day she braced herself for a special
edition of *The Muskrat Times*—an edition that
would carry across the front page a picture of her
and Steve Urkel looking like Scarlett O'Hara and
Rhett Butler locked in a passionate embrace.

Every morning, she had awakened with a shud-
der as she imagined the looks she would get from
her fellow students when they got their copies of
the paper: shock, pity, revulsion. And surely, after
seeing such a picture, no one would be able to
bring themselves to vote for her. Lounging in

Steve Urkel's arms was far from presidential behavior!

But why hadn't that special edition been published? She had a feeling that Steve Urkel was behind this. He had certainly been quiet and secretive all week.

In spite of Cassie Lynn's attempt to drag her into the gutter, Laura was basically pleased with the way she had waged her campaign. She had based that campaign on the idea of student empowerment—the idea that students were citizens of their school with a rightful say in how that school was run. The issues she emphasized had been the poor heating in the girls' locker room, the poor lighting in the parking lot, and the lack of facilities for the handicapped.

Mr. Shimata had stood next to the voting booth all morning while students waited on line to file their ballots. He was pleased to see that the student turnout was excellent, the best in years. As an ex-social studies teacher, Mr. Shimata loved nothing better than to see democracy in action.

Before the last class of the day, the students gathered in the main hall and waited for the principal's announcement. Surrounded by her friends, Laura stood nervously, waiting to see if all her hard work would pay off. She felt she had given it her best shot. She had campaigned hard, made her views known to one and all, stood toe-to-toe with Cassie Lynn and debated the issues. There was only one thing still puzzling Laura, still nagging at her.

What had happened to the photograph Cassie Lynn had threatened to publish? Laura had even prepared a cover story explaining the truth in the event the photo showed up in *The Muskrat Times*. Even though the truth sounded like a lie, she knew the other kids considered her honest.

"Nice sweater." Maxine's voice drew Laura away from her thoughts.

"Thanks," she said. "Mother Winslow knitted it for me."

It was a picture of a lioness done against the school colors. It *was* a nice sweater, even if she didn't win. Laura closed her eyes. She felt almost faint with anticipation. She heard the sound of her heart—it drowned out the buzzing of the other students around her. It wasn't until this moment that she realized just how badly she wanted to win. It wasn't the office or the telephone she wanted. It was the opportunity to make things happen, to give her fellow students a voice in how things were run.

"Your attention, please," Mr. Shimata said over the PA system. "I have the results of this morning's election for Student Council president."

The din in the hallway rose. Laura felt

someone squeeze her hand. She turned to find Steve standing by her side, staring up at the speaker. His eyes were wide and hopeful. It was hard to stay mad at a guy who cared so much. If she lost, she thought, she would be as disappointed for him as she would be for herself. He had worked so hard.

"Cassie Lynn Nubbles," the principal said, " . . . three hundred and twenty votes."

The crowd gasped in surprise. Laura's heart lurched. She felt a lump rising in her throat. In a matter of seconds, she would have to face Cassie Lynn and offer up her congratulations.

Cassie, smiling smugly, went over to her locker and opened it. She reached in, grabbed two pompoms, and prepared herself to cheer her own victory.

"Laura Winslow," the principal continued, " . . . three hundred and fifty-two! Laura Winslow is our new president!"

The students cheered loudly. Before Steve knew it, Laura had thrown her arms around him and was hugging him. Hugging *him*! He could scarcely believe it. He hugged her back. For one wild moment, he actually thought she was going to kiss him! But that moment faded when Laura suddenly realized what she was doing. Embarrassed, she backed away from him.

"Sorry," Steve said.

"I lost my head," Laura stammered.

"Wasn't thinking," Steve said.

A humiliated Cassie Lynn flung her pom-poms back in her locker and slammed the door.

Laura still couldn't get over it. She shook her head in astonishment. "I won, Steve. I really won!"

"I knew you could do it," Steve said, staring at her in dewy-eyed admiration. "Didn't I say that you could do it all along?"

Laura smiled at him. "You sure did, Steve. You never lost faith in me."

"How could I?" Steve said. "You're my bright angel."

"I still don't understand why Cassie Lynn changed her mind about publishing the picture of us," Laura said, eyeing him suspiciously. She couldn't help but feel that Steve had had something to do with it. "Steve," she said, bearing down on him, "you didn't by any chance have anything to do with Cassie Lynn changing her mind?"

Steve backed away from her. "Well, Laura," he said, not meeting her eye, "stuck-up princesses are unpredictable."

Laura shrugged and dropped it. "Maybe Cassie Lynn has a shred of decency after all," she said thoughtfully.

Just then Cassie Lynn marched over to Laura

and snarled, "I want a recount, you lucky little creep."

Laura and Steve turned to each other and grinned knowingly.

Steve laughed. "Maybe not," he said.

"Come on," Cassie Lynn said to Becky Sue, "let's get out of here."

But Becky Sue turned her nose up at the suggestion. "Get lost... *loser!*"

Cassie Lynn flounced off down the hall alone.

Laura turned again to Steve, this time with a look of pure gratitude. "I really want to thank you for all your help," she said shyly. "I couldn't have done it without you. You were the best campaign manager a girl ever had."

Steve scuffed his saddle shoes. "It was your charisma that did it. I'm just your humble servant."

"I'd like to repay you somehow," Laura said. "Maybe I could give you an exclusive interview for the newspaper?...Give you your own chair in my new office?...Take down all the posters myself?"

"Actually...," Steve began. Then he stopped. *Forget it*, he told himself. It was asking too much.

"Come on, Steve," Laura said. "Out with it. What can I do for you?"

"Well...," he tried again, "maybe you

could...find it within yourself...to give me the merest, tiniest, eeniest, beeniest little...kiss?"

Laura raised an eyebrow and was about to tell him to forget it. But when she thought about it, it really wasn't asking all that much, especially considering all he had done for her. In fact, one kiss was a pretty cheap price to pay for all those hours and all that good advice.

"I'm not making any promises," she said, "but if you'll pick me up tonight at seven o'clock, we can go to Rachel's Place and discuss it—over a victory cheeseburger and fries."

"And a Laura-palooza for dessert?" Steve asked hopefully.

She grinned. "That's on me."

"Madam President, you're too kind," her manager said. Laughing the Urkel laugh—*snort, snort, snicker, snicker*—he began taking down posters. He intended to save every last one of them, for his memory album.